Double Trouble

Written by Anna Milbourne

Illustrated by Tamsin Hinrichsen

How this book works

The story of **Double Trouble** has been written for you to read with your child. You take turns to read:

You read these words.

Your child reads these words.

You don't have to finish the story in one session. If your child is getting tired, put a marker in the page and come back to it later.

You can find out more about helping your child with this book, and with reading in general, on pages 30-31.

Double Trouble

Turn the page to start the story.

Here's a twin and here's his brother.
Can you tell one from the other?
Not too many people can.

I am Dan.

And, you know, it's such a shame:
One twin always gets the blame
For the things the other did.

Dan!
Dan!
I am Sid!

Sporty Dan just loves to run,
Sid thinks eating's much more fun...
Who stole cakes from sleepy Stan?

Sid! Sid!
I am Dan!

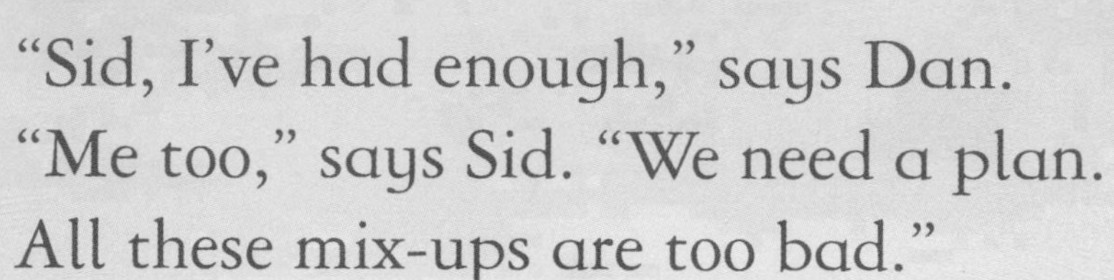

"Sid, I've had enough," says Dan.
"Me too," says Sid. "We need a plan.
All these mix-ups are too bad."

Sid is sad.

Dan is mad.

The twins think hard. How can they show
Which one is which, so people know?

They buy some paint,
take off the lid...

Tip it, Sid!

They paint each other red and green.
Now the difference can be seen.
Wasn't that a clever plan?

Is it Dan?
It is Dan!

It all works well until, one day,
A friend arrives from far away –
A naughty monkey on a trip.

Tap, tap, tap.
It is Pip.

One morning they go out to play
And Pip picks up the hose to spray...

Oh no!
Who mixed up Dan and Sid?

I did!

Puzzle 1

Look at the pictures together and try retelling the story.

1.

2.

3.

4.

5.

6.

Can you think of any other ways for the twins to show everyone who's who?

Puzzle 2

Choose the right words for each picture.

1.

Sid is pad.	Sid is sad.

2.

Dan is mad.	Dan is man.

3.

Sip it, Dan!

Tip it, Dan!

4.

Tap, tap, tap.

Tan, tan, tan.

Puzzle 3

Can you sort these words into two groups of rhymes?

sad	dip
tip	mad
pad	nip
dad	sip

Answers to puzzles

Puzzle 1

Use this puzzle to check that your child has understood the story, and have fun discussing how the twins could show everyone who's who.

If your child isn't sure what to say, try asking leading questions such as, "Who's this? What are they doing now?" (Of course, there is more than one possible answer.)

Puzzle 2

1. Sid is sad.
2. Dan is mad.
3. Tip it, Dan!
4. Tap, tap, tap.

Puzzle 3

sad dip
mad tip
pad nip
dad sip

Guidance notes

Usborne Very First Reading is a series of books, specially developed for children who are learning to read. In the early books in the series, you and your child take turns to read, and your child steadily builds the knowledge and confidence to read alone.

The words for your child to read in **Double Trouble** use only these eight letters:

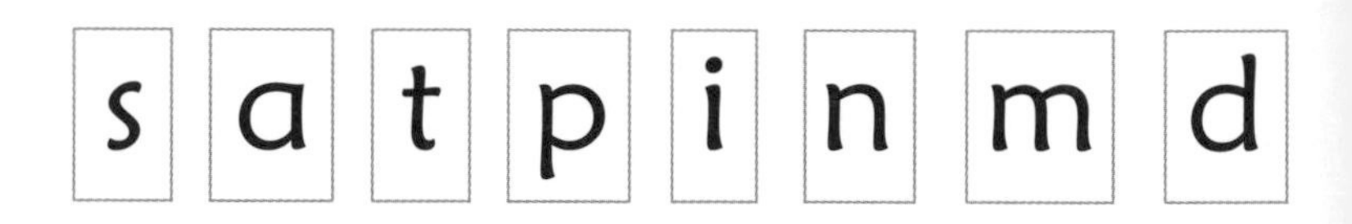

These are often the first letters that children learn to read at school. With just eight letters, your child can already start reading simple words and sentences. Later books in the series gradually introduce more letters, sounds and spelling patterns, while reinforcing the ones your child already knows.

You'll find lots more information about the structure of the series, advice on helping your child with reading, extra practice activities and games on the Very First Reading website,* **www.usborne.com/veryfirstreading**

*US readers go to **www.veryfirstreading.com**

Some questions and answers

- **Why do I need to read with my child?**
  Sharing stories and taking turns makes reading an enjoyable and fun activity for children. It also helps them to develop confidence and reading stamina, and to take part in an exciting story using very few words.
- **When is a good time to read?**
  Choose a time when you are both relaxed, but not too tired, and there are no distractions. Only read for as long as your child wants to – you can always try again another day.
- **What if my child gets stuck?**
  Don't simply read the problem word yourself, but prompt your child and try to find the right answer together. Similarly, if your child makes a mistake, go back and look at the word together. Don't forget to give plenty of praise and encouragement.
- **We've finished, now what do we do?**
  It's a good idea to read the story several times to give your child more practice and confidence. Then you can try reading **Pirate Pat** at the same level or, when your child is ready, go on to Book 2 in the series.

Edited by Jenny Tyler, Lesley Sims
and Mairi Mackinnon
Designed by Caroline Spatz

First published in 2011 by Usborne Publishing Ltd., Usborne House, 83-85 Saffron Hill, London EC1N 8RT, England. www.usborne.com

UE. First published in America in 2011.